YELLOW BIRD AND ME

JOYCE HANSEN

CLARION BOOKS

NEW YORK

For my students
and for the
Nataki Talibah Schoolhouse

Clarion Books
a Houghton Mifflin Company imprint
215 Park Avenue South, New York, NY 10003
Copyright © 1986 by Joyce Hansen
All rights reserved.
For information about permission to reproduce
selections from this book write to Permissions,
Houghton Mifflin Company, 215 Park Avenue South, New York, NY 10003.
Printed in the USA

Library of Congress Cataloging in Publication Data. Hansen, Joyce. Yellow Bird and me. Sequel to: The gift-giver. Summary: Doris becomes friends with Yellow Bird as she helps him with his studies and his part in the school play and discovers that he has a problem known as dyslexia. 1. Children's stories, American. [1. Friendship—Fiction. 2. Dyslexia—Fiction. 3. Schools—Fiction] I. Title. PZ7.H19825Ye 1986 [Fic] 85—484 ISBN 0-89919-335-8
PA ISBN 0-395-55388-1
QUM 20 19 18 17 16